THREE BALLS OF WOOL

(CAN CHANGE THE WORLD)

In association with:

www.enchantedlionbooks.com
www.amnestyusa.org

First American Edition published in 2017 by Enchanted Lion Books,
67 West Street, 317A, Brooklyn, New York 11222
English-language translation copyright © 2017 by Lyn Miller-Lachmann
English-language edition copyright © 2017 by Enchanted Lion Books
Originally published in Portugal by Planeta Tangerina © 2015
as *Com 3 Novelos (O Mundo Dá Muitas Voltas)*
All rights reserved under International and Pan-American Copyright Conventions
A CIP record is on file with the Library of Congress
ISBN: 978-1-59270-220-6
Printed in China by RR Donnelley Asia Printing Solutions

First Printing

THREE BALLS OF WOOL (CAN CHANGE THE WORLD)

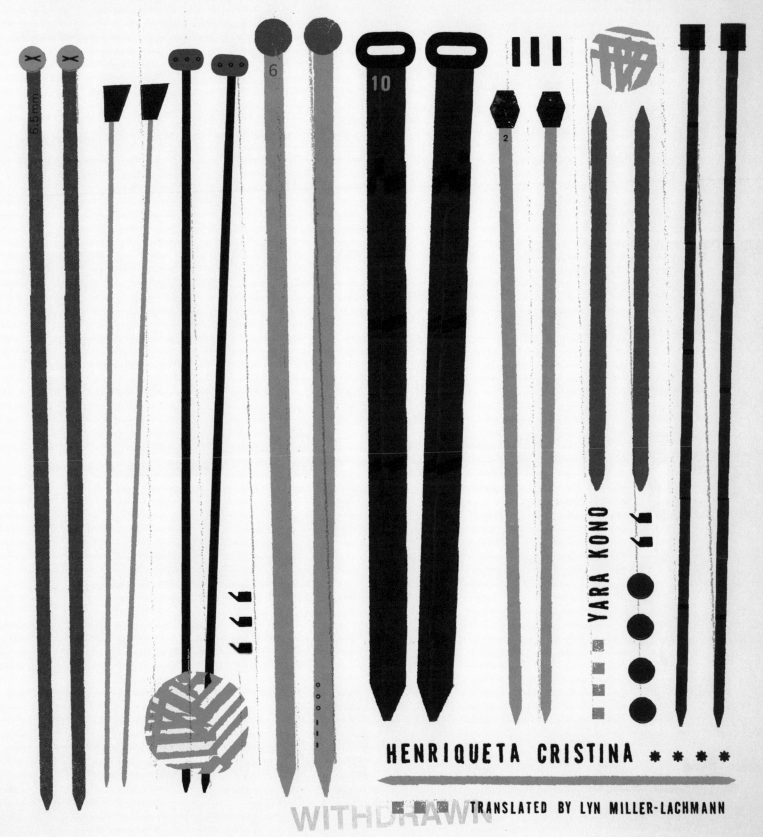

YARA KONO

HENRIQUETA CRISTINA ✳ ✳ ✳ ✳

TRANSLATED BY LYN MILLER-LACHMANN

ENCHANTED LION BOOKS

FOREWORD

In 1961, British lawyer Peter Benenson was on the London Underground when he read a small item in the newspaper about two Portuguese students who were jailed for raising their glasses in a toast to freedom. Outraged by such injustice, this modest lawyer was spurred into action. He submitted an appeal to *The Observer*, urging readers to write letters on behalf of "prisoners of conscience" around the world. His appeal was published. It sparked an international campaign to protect human rights, and with that, Amnesty International was born.

Three Balls of Wool is a timely reminder that defending and protecting the basic human rights of all people—from the freedom of expression to the right to seek asylum from persecution in other countries—is a responsibility that belongs to all of us. Today, we are in the midst of a global refugee and migrant crisis. For these individuals, the decision to leave home and flee their countries is a matter of life and death that follows from political unrest, civil conflict, social marginalization, economic insecurity, and environmental disaster. Many migrants and refugees leave their countries because they do not have adequate access to food, water, or shelter, or because the safety of their family is at risk. Every story of upheaval is different, but the decision to leave is never made lightly.

The Universal Declaration of Human Rights (UDHR) provides us with a framework of rights that apply to every human being, regardless of race, color, religion, sex, national origin, sexual orientation, gender identity, disability, or age. These are the fundamental rights with which we all are born.

The fact of our own freedoms doesn't give us the right to impinge on the freedoms of any other person. Hatred, bigotry, wrongful judgment, and violence in word and deed must therefore be rejected at every turn. Rather, we must seek to advance the cause of human freedom by engaging in civil society to safeguard our freedoms and human dignity.

The world Mr. Benenson was born into was one in which not a single international human rights treaty existed. *The Universal Declaration of Human Rights* had yet to be written. There were no human rights organizations. Civil society had yet to be born.

But today, Amnesty International is a global movement of more than seven million people which takes injustice personally and is committed to shaping a world where human rights—as enshrined in the UDHR and other international standards—are enjoyed by all. And because the institutions of civil society are independent of any government, political ideology, economic interest, or religion, they are able to defend citizens against their governments and against all abuses of power, no matter where they originate.

Along with other international aid groups, Amnesty International works to protect and empower people in the following ways: defending the rights of migrants and refugees; combating discrimination; opposing the death penalty; and protecting sexual and reproductive rights. It campaigns to bring torturers to justice, change oppressive laws, and free people who are jailed simply for voicing their opinion.

As communities, it is vital that we never cease to defend justice, human rights, and common human decency. Our words and deeds can make a real difference in the lives of other people, so our intent must be to never harm through them. Respect, fairness, truthfulness, thoughtfulness, and kindness make the world a better place.

Cynthia Gabriel Walsh
Senior Director, Organizing Unit,
Amnesty International USA

When I was eight years old, I lived in a warm, sunny country.
It was also one where few children went to school.

My parents worried so much that lines appeared
on their foreheads. They said words I didn't understand.
Words they whispered to each other, like:
"Ignorance." "Fear." "War." "Prison."

One day I heard them say, "Exile." The line on my father's
forehead deepened. The next day we left before dawn.

We arrived in our new country at the end of summer.
At first, the language sounded strange.
My mom said that children learn new languages
faster than grownups.
She was right, as always.

Our new country was very different from our old one.
It was clean and tidy.

"Here there are no poor people and all the children go
to school." My mom repeated this often.

Once we were settled, I noticed my
father's frown had disappeared.

When autumn arrived, I started school.
School was a large, gray building with tall windows.
It looked like a shoebox lying on its side, right in the
middle of our neighborhood. Our apartment building
looked like a bunch of gray shoeboxes stacked one
on top of the other.

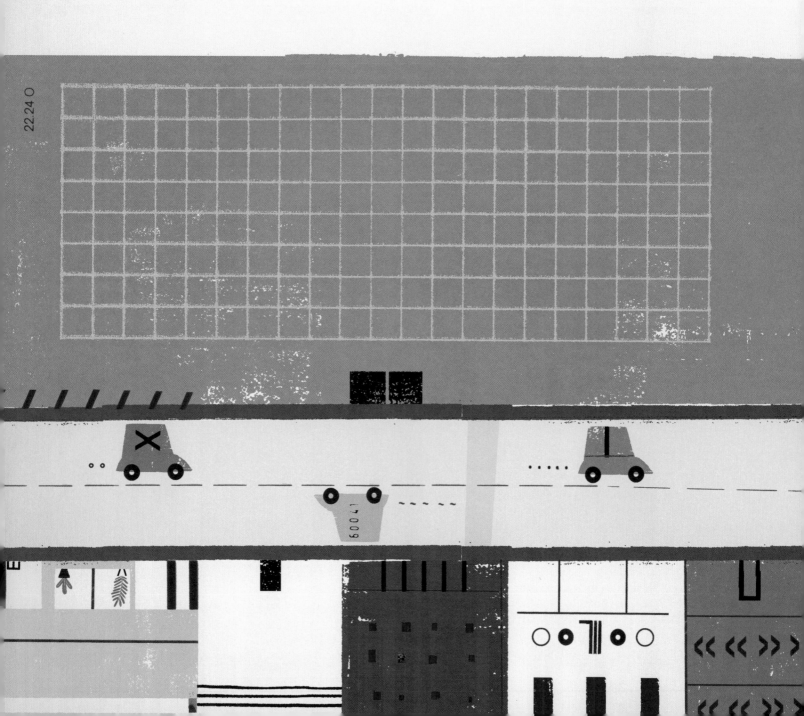

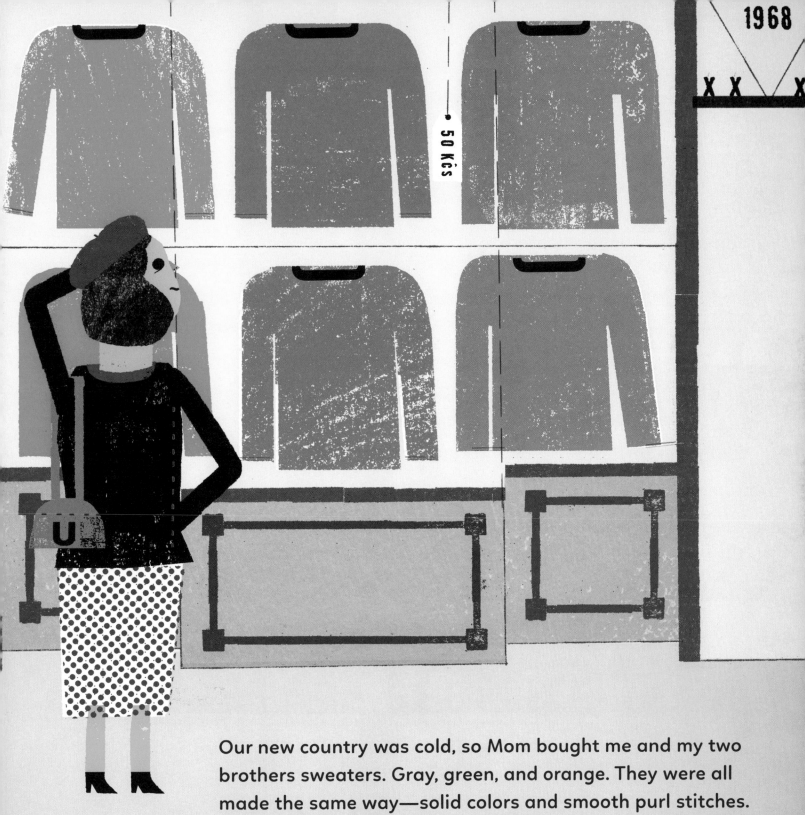

1968

50 Kčs

Our new country was cold, so Mom bought me and my two brothers sweaters. Gray, green, and orange. They were all made the same way—solid colors and smooth purl stitches. (Mom knew everything about knitting.)

"It's strange how sweaters come in only three colors here," she said. "It must be the fashion."

But I didn't think it was strange, because everyone dressed exactly the same already. Every morning, the neighborhood filled with mothers and fathers dressed in the same brown clothes on their way to work. Children wore gray, green, and orange sweaters to school.

We followed each other in an orderly way, almost as silent as the street lamps.

"They look like an army marching in their uniforms," Mom whispered to Dad. By late autumn, a tiny frown line had appeared on her forehead.

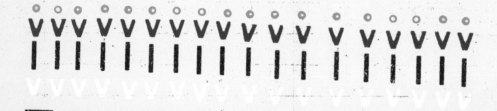

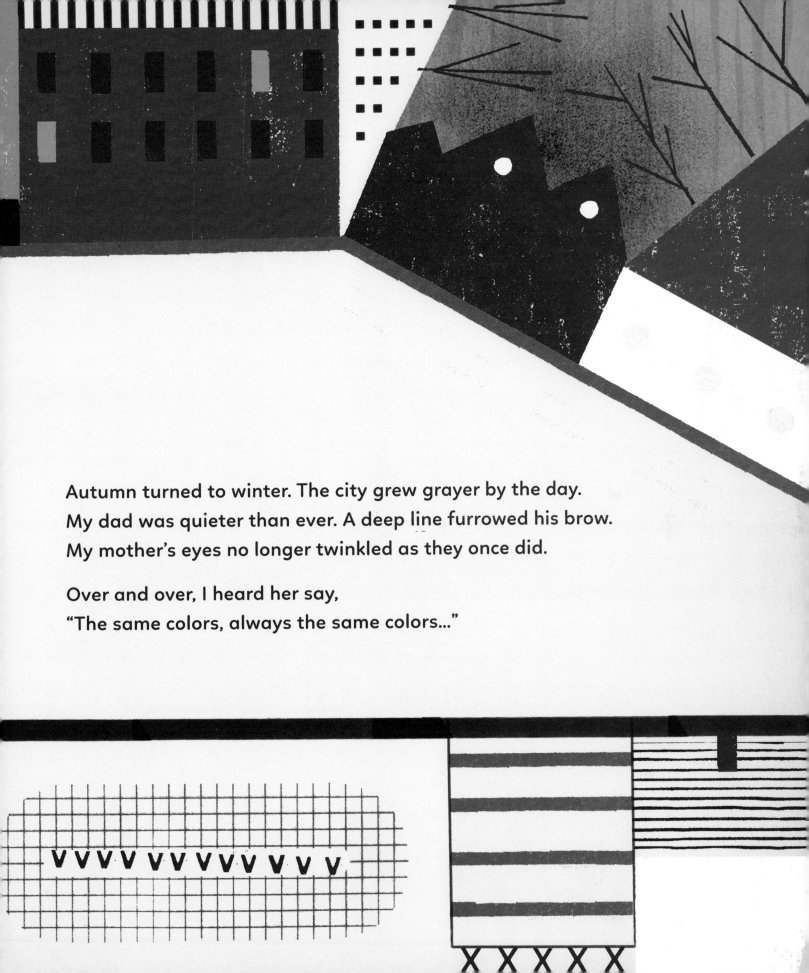

Autumn turned to winter. The city grew grayer by the day.
My dad was quieter than ever. A deep line furrowed his brow.
My mother's eyes no longer twinkled as they once did.

Over and over, I heard her say,
"The same colors, always the same colors..."

I missed the sun, my friends, my grandparents, and my cats.

"Mom, what happened to the litter that was born the day before we left?"

"Oh, let's not worry about that. Kittens are born here too," Mom replied.

Afterward, she braided my hair and her gentle touch put everything right inside me. I think it was then that she came up with her plan.

She started with a gray sweater.
I stayed up late, mesmerized
by her quick fingers.

First, she snipped a thread.
Then she began to pull.
She unraveled the sweater
like a movie played backward,
winding the yarn around
her left hand. She formed
it into a perfect ball and
dropped it into the basket.

She did the same thing
with an orange sweater
and a green one.

When the basket held three balls of
wool, Mom picked up her needles,
hung a loop of yarn around her neck,
and began to knit.

Every night for the next few weeks her needles
clicked and flashed: knit-purl, purl-knit, twist, reverse.
Mom knew the names of all the stitches.

The first sweater she knitted had orange, green, and gray stripes.
It was beautiful, and she was making it for me!

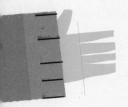

Her needles clicked and flashed. I loved the dance of her needles
and recited the mysterious names of the stitches over and over:
knit-purl, purl-knit, shell, cable, slip stitch, seed.

X X X X X X X X X X X X X X X X X X X X X X

UUUUUUU UUUU UU UU UUUUUL

O O O O O O O O O O O O O O

Next, she knitted sweaters for my brothers.
One had gray, orange, and green zigzags.
The other had gray and orange squares
with a green border.

By the time Mom finished,
winter was almost over.

The following Sunday we went for a walk in our new sweaters.
We strolled through the neighborhood and arrived
at an enormous square, where children in solid orange, green,
and gray sweaters were chasing pigeons. Mom sat down
on a bench with her knitting. This time she was making
a sweater with green and orange diamonds.

I ran towards the pigeons with my brothers. Suddenly, I felt
a strange silence all around us. Everyone was staring. The
children came closer to get a better look.

"What's that sweater?" one girl asked.
"My mother made it." My voice grew stronger.
"Come see," I said, waving towards my mom.

The following Sunday, needles clicked and flashed all
across the square, as they did every Sunday after that.
Knit, purl, cable, slip stitch, seed.

Now the park wasn't just full of mothers, fathers, and children,
but also of needles and wool. Families came from near and far.
They brought sweaters, snipped threads, and unraveled yarn.
Needles clicked and flashed, fashioning squares, rectangles,
stripes, birds, and flowers.

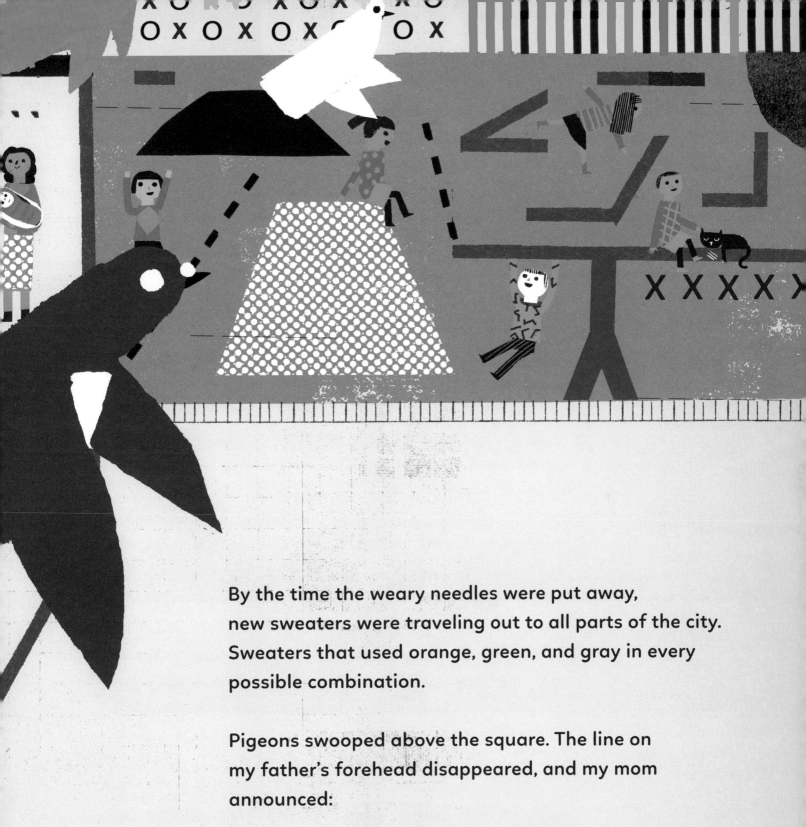

By the time the weary needles were put away,
new sweaters were traveling out to all parts of the city.
Sweaters that used orange, green, and gray in every
possible combination.

Pigeons swooped above the square. The line on
my father's forehead disappeared, and my mom
announced:

"Spring is here!"

From 1926 to 1974, the right-wing dictatorship of António de Oliveira Salazar (1926–1968) and Marcelo Caetano (1968–1974) ruled Portugal. During those 48 years, the Portuguese people could not vote in free elections, the press was censored, and those who criticized the government often ended up in prison or expelled from the country. The fascist regime, called the *Estado Novo* (New State), restricted the rights of women and offered free schooling for only a few years. As a result, illiteracy, a major problem through Portugal's history, remained far higher than in neighboring countries into the 1970s.

Although Portugal remained neutral in the Second World War (1939–1945), Salazar and his generals sympathized with the Nazis, who they saw as the strongest force against Communism. During the Cold War (1945–1989), Portugal outlawed the Communist Party and joined the North Atlantic Treaty Organization (NATO) against the Soviet Union and its satellite states. Salazar and Caetano accused their opponents of being Communists, whether or not it was true, because it was a way of discrediting them. Indeed, many of their opponents did not believe in one of the central tenets of Communism, which is that the state should own all property. Others did, however, advocate for a more equitable distribution of land and wealth because under the *Estado Novo*, Portugal was a highly stratified society, with a small privileged class and a large mass of rural and urban poor. Those who desired greater fairness saw Communism as a means of addressing poverty, inequality, and the lack of education.

Three Balls of Wool is based on the story of a Portuguese family that fled the dictatorship in the late 1960s and lived in exile in Algeria, Romania, and finally Czechoslovakia. Sadly, they did not find the freedom they sought anywhere they went. In this story, the wearing of only gray, green, and orange sweaters was invented by the author to symbolize the conformity demanded by Communism, along with the severe shortages characteristic of those regimes. In 1968, the family actively participated in what is known as the Prague Spring, a period of somewhat greater openness and freedom in Communist Czechoslovakia that coincides with the final part of this book. As it turned out, the Prague Spring would last only a few months before Soviet troops invaded and regained control. It took 21 more years for the Velvet Revolution of 1989 to put an end to one-party rule in Czechoslovakia, and for the first democratic elections to take place. In 1993, Czechoslovakia divided into two separate democratic countries, the Czech Republic and Slovakia. Nowadays, children in both countries can wear sweaters of any color in whatever pattern they choose.

In Portugal, the dictatorship ended on April 25, 1974, with the Carnation Revolution, a peaceful uprising in which the army and the people took to the streets to reclaim their freedom. But it was even before then, during a period known as the Marcellist Spring, that the family returned home, able to do so because of Salazar's resignation for health reasons, and the Caetano government's temporary lifting of political restrictions. Today, Portugal has a democratically elected government and every child goes to school.

X X X X X X X X X X X X X X X X X X X X X X X X X X X X X

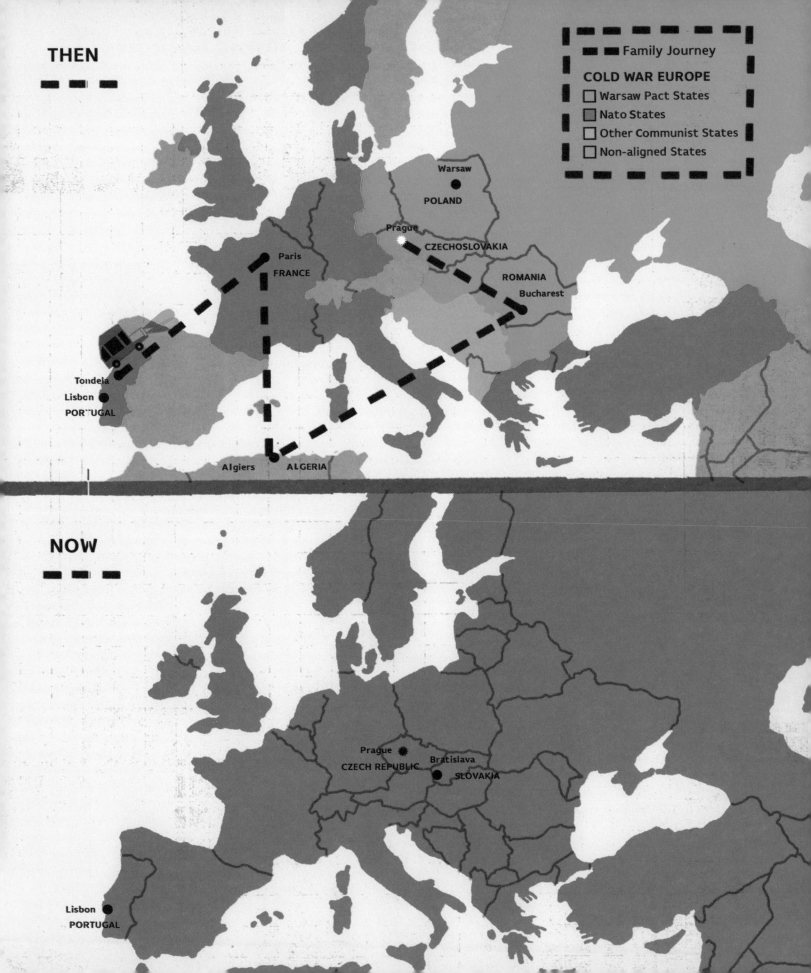

THEN

- - - -

Warsaw

POLAND

Prague

CZECHOSLOVAKIA

Paris

FRANCE

ROMANIA

Bucharest

Tondela

Lisbon

PORTUGAL

Algiers   **ALGERIA**

NOW

- - -

Prague

CZECH REPUBLIC   Bratislava   **SLOVAKIA**

Lisbon

PORTUGAL

The Universal Declaration of Human Rights

Article 1
All human beings are born free and equal in rights. Endowed with reason and conscience, we should act towards one another in a spirit of kindness and community.

Article 2
Each of us has all the rights and freedoms set forth in this declaration, regardless of race, color, sex, language, religion, belief, origin, property, nationality, or other status.

Article 3
Each of us has the right to life, liberty, and personal safety.

Article 4
No one shall be held in slavery or servitude.

Article 5
No one shall be subjected to torture or to cruel or degrading treatment or punishment.

Article 6
We all have the right to be recognized throughout the world as a person before the law.

Article 7
We all are equal before the law and are entitled to equal protection and treatment under it.

Article 8
If your legal rights are violated, you have the right to a fair, qualified judge to uphold your rights.

Article 9
No one shall be subjected to groundless arrest, detention, or exile.

Article 10
If you are accused of a crime, you have the right to a fair and public hearing.

Article 11
1) If charged with an offense, you shall be considered innocent until proven guilty in a fair and public trial.

2) You shall not be punished for something that was not considered a crime at the time you did it.

Article 12
Each of us has the right to legal protection against groundless interference of privacy, family, home, and mail, as well as against attacks on our honor and reputation.

Article 13
1) Each of us has the right to come and go as we wish within our own country.

2) Each of us has the right to leave and return to our own country.

Article 14
1) If you are threatened and at risk, you have the right to go to another country to ask for protection as a refugee.

2) You shall lose this right if you have committed a serious crime.

Article 15
1) Everyone has the right to a nationality and to belong to a country.

2) No one shall have their nationality arbitrarily taken from them, nor denied the right to change their nationality.

Article 16
1) When you are of legal age, you have the right to marry and have a family without any limitations based on race, nationality, or religion. Both partners have the same rights in marriage and in divorce.

2) You shall not be forced into marriage.

3) Every family shall be entitled to protection by the government.

Article 17
1) Each of us has the right to own things on our own as well as with others.

2) No one has the right to simply take these things away from you.

Article 18
Each of us has the right to freedom of thought, conscience, and religion. This right includes the freedom to change religions or beliefs and to practice publicly or in private.

Article 19
Each of us has the right to freedom of opinion and expression, including the right to share our views with others, regardless of geographic boundaries.

Article 20
1) Each of us has the right to meet peacefully with others.

2) No one may force you to belong to a group or association.

Article 21

1) Each of us has the right to take part in the government of our country, directly or through freely chosen representatives.

2) Each of us has the right to pursue public service.

3) The will of the people is the basis of government. This shall be expressed through regularly held free and fair elections.

Article 22

As a member of a society, each of us has the right to security and is entitled to the rights necessary for human dignity and personal development.

Article 23

1) Each of us has the right to work, to a fair and decent work environment, and to protection against unemployment.

2) Each of us has the right to equal pay for equal work.

3) Each of us who works has the right to a living wage that ensures an existence worthy of human dignity.

4) Each of us has the right to form and join unions to protect our interests.

Article 24

Each of us has the right to rest and leisure. Work days should not be too long, and we should be able to take regular, paid vacations.

Article 25

1) Each of us has the right to a standard of living adequate for the well-being of self and family, including food, clothing, housing, medical care, and necessary social services. We have the right to assistance if we are out of or unable to work.

2) Mothers and children shall be entitled to special assistance.

Article 26

1) Each of us has the right to go to school. Primary schooling should be free and required. You should be able to learn a profession or continue your studies as far as you can.

2) At school, you should be able to develop all your talents and learn to respect others, whatever their race, religion, or nationality.

3) Your parents should have a say in the kind of education you receive.

Article 27

1) You have the right to participate in the traditions and learning of your community, to enjoy the arts and to benefit from scientific progress.

2) If you are an artist, writer, or scientist, your work should be protected and you should be able to benefit from it.

Article 28

You have the right to live in the kind of world where you and all people can enjoy these rights and freedoms.

Article 29

1) Each of us is rooted within a community and we have responsibilities to that community.

2) The laws should support mutual respect and serve as a guarantee of our human rights.

3) Human rights and freedoms should be defined in accordance with the principles of the United Nations.

Article 30

This declaration does not give any government, group, or person the right to infringe upon the freedoms of any other.